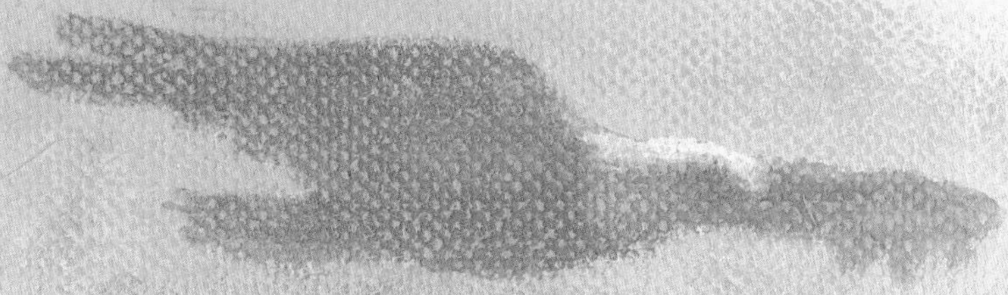

Trouble Coming!

Christine Harris

Illustrated by
Hamish Blakely

TED SMART

'Trouble coming,' croaked the eagle.
'I can see it.'
  'Trouble coming,' growled the bobcat.
'I can hear it.'

'Trouble coming,' sniffed the otter.
'I can smell it.'

'Trouble? Is
that why you're
swimming?' Mother
'Gator asked
the otter.

'And is that why you're running?'
Mother 'Gator asked the bobcat.

'You see trouble, Mister Eagle?
What's the trouble? Can't you tell me?'
 'I see lightning start that fire,'
croaked the eagle.

'The fire's spreading. Hear it crackling!' growled the bobcat.
'Smell that smoke! The fire is nearer,' warned the otter.

'Fire will kill us if we stay here.

Swim behind me! Hurry, hurry.
Trouble coming!'

Mother 'Gator wasn't listening.

'I'll go this way,' she decided.
'I have children. I must save them.'

'Here's the nest I laid the eggs in.
I must wait till all my eggs hatch.
Children, children – are you ready?
Hurry, hurry. Trouble coming!'

One by one, her children joined her. 'But what is it? What's the trouble?'

'Can't you smell it, hear it, see it?
FIRE! FIRE!' roared Mother 'Gator.

'But there's a pool that I've been digging, with my tail I've made it deeper. Hurry, hurry. Trouble coming!'

'We'll be safe here,
underwater.'

High above,
the eagle circled.

'Rain clouds gathering,'
croaked the eagle.

'Rain is falling,
I can hear it.'

'The fire is dying. Rain has stopped it. Trouble going, trouble going, trouble going . . .'

'TROUBLE GONE!'

With thanks to Peter – C.H.
To Juanita the alligator: never have I had
such an understanding model – H.B.

TROUBLE COMING!

This edition produced for The Book People Ltd,
Hall Wood Avenue, Haydock, St Helens, WA11 9UL

First published in Great Britain by Hutchinson,
an imprint of Random House Children's Books

This edition published 2003

1 3 5 7 9 10 8 6 4 2

Text © Christine Harris, 2003
Illustrations © Hamish Blakely, 2003

RANDOM HOUSE CHILDREN'S BOOKS
61–63 Uxbridge Road, London W5 5SA
A division of The Random House Group Ltd

RANDOM HOUSE AUSTRALIA (PTY) LTD
20 Alfred Street, Milsons Point, Sydney,
New South Wales 2061, Australia

RANDOM HOUSE NEW ZEALAND LTD
18 Poland Road, Glenfield, Auckland 10, New Zealand

RANDOM HOUSE (PTY) LTD
Endulini, 5A Jubilee Road, Parktown 2193, South Africa

THE RANDOM HOUSE GROUP Limited Reg. No. 954009

A CIP catalogue record for this book is available from the British Library.

Printed in Hong Kong